D0437520

Savannah the Zebra Fairy

To Myla, from the fairies

Special thanks to Rachel Elliot

ISBN 978-0-545-70853-1

12 11 10 9 8 7 6 5 4 3 2 1 15 16 17 18 19/0

Printed in the U.S.A. 40

First Scholastic printing, January 2015

Savannah the Zebra Fairy

by Daisy Meadows

SCHOLASTIC INC.

The Fairyland Palace
Meadow
Stream
Beehive
Arctic Tundra
Eucalyptus Forest
Tropical Waterfall

Wild Woods
Nature
Reserve
Watering Hole
Pagoda

Jack Frost's
Ice Castle
To Jack Frost's Zoo
Desert Oasis

I love animals—yes, I do,
I want my very own private zoo!
I'll capture all the animals one by one,
With fairy magic to help me get it done!

A koala, a tiger, an Arctic fox,
I'll keep them in cages with giant locks.
Every kind of animal will be there,
A panda, a meerkat, a honey bear.
The animals will be my property,
I'll be master of my own menagerie!

Contents

A Deer Display

"I wonder what junior ranger badges we'll earn today," said Rachel Walker as she got out of the car at the Wild Woods Nature Reserve.

"I hope we'll be spending time with the animals again," said her best friend Kirsty Tate. "Since the fairies gave us the gift of being able to understand what animals say, I want to be with them all the time!"

The girls smiled at each other happily. As friends of Fairyland, they were used to magical adventures. But this summer they were having a non-magical adventure, too. They were spending a week as volunteer junior rangers at Wild Woods Nature Reserve. Every day, the junior rangers earned badges for their backpacks by doing jobs around the reserve. Rachel and Kirsty had already earned three badges.

"This week is going so fast," said Rachel. "I can't believe it's already our fourth day!"

"Look, there's Becky," said Kirsty, seeing the head of the reserve walking toward them. "Come on, let's find out what she wants us to do today."

The girls waved good-bye to Mrs.

Tate, who had driven them to the nature reserve.

"Good morning, girls!" said Becky. "I've got an exciting job for you. I want you to feed our herd of deer. They're some of the sweetest animals on the reserve, and there's a baby fawn that's especially cute. But he's very shy, so you might not see him."

The girls could hardly believe their ears. The beautiful deer were one of the main visitor attractions at the reserve.

"Really?" Rachel gasped. "Thank you, Becky!"

"It's like a dream come true!" said Kirsty.

"Well, let's get started, then!" said Becky with a laugh.

She led the girls over to where four large buckets were waiting on the ground.

"These are full of deer feed," said Becky.

"What do the deer eat?" asked Kirsty, looking into the buckets.

"It's a special mixture of fruit and grasses," Becky told them.

"The visitors love to watch them being fed every day."

"Why do the deer have to be fed by humans?" Rachel asked. "Isn't there enough food for them growing at the nature reserve?"

"That's a really good question," said Becky. "There's plenty of food for the deer growing here, but we do a special daily feeding display for the visitors so they can see the animals close-up."

Carrying two buckets each, the girls followed Becky to a pretty meadow, full of clover and buttercups. On the far side of the meadow was a leafy forest, and a fence surrounded the other three sides. There were lots of people standing beside the fence. They looked excited and hopeful.

“Look, the visitors are gathering already,” said Becky. “I’ll go over and talk to them while you scatter the food around. The deer will be here soon—they know when it’s feeding time!”

She walked over to the fence, and Rachel and Kirsty made their way slowly through the meadow toward the woods, scattering the deer feed as they went.

“My heart’s thumping like crazy,” said Kirsty in a whisper. “We’re actually going to see real-life deer!”

“Look!” said Rachel in a thrilled voice.

Two deer were stepping out of the woods and into the meadow. One was a female with a velvet-soft coat, and the other was a buck with large antlers. They moved with incredible grace, and they shyly blinked their big eyes as they looked at the

girls. Kirsty smiled and scattered a little more food. The animals moved closer. Then more of the herd came out from between the trees. Soon the girls were surrounded by lots of deer wanting food.

"Listen," said Kirsty. "They're whispering to one another!"

"Not many visitors today," the girls heard one buck saying to another.

"Eat up, everybody," said a third.

"*Mmm*, scrumptious clover," murmured a young female deer behind Rachel.

"I'm so glad that you like it," said Rachel in a soft voice.

The deer all perked up their ears and stared at her with interest.

"How unusual," said an older female. "Humans who really know how to communicate!"

"We're friends with the fairies," Kirsty explained to them. "They gave us the magical power to talk to animals."

"It was the best gift ever," Rachel added.

"Yes," said Kirsty thoughtfully, turning to her best friend. "But we shouldn't forget *why* they gave it to us. We promised to help protect the animals from Jack Frost and his goblins! We can't let him take animals from the wild—you can't just collect animals like that."

On their first day at Wild Woods Nature Reserve, the girls had traveled to Fairyland and met the Baby Animal Rescue Fairies, who looked after animals in both Fairyland and in the human world. While they were there, Jack Frost had stolen the fairies' magic key chains and ordered his goblins to bring him lots of animals from the human world. He wanted to put them in a private zoo for

his own selfish enjoyment. Kirsty and Rachel had vowed to stop him, and the fairies had given them the power to talk to animals.

"We've already saved a panda, a tiger, and a meerkat," said Rachel. "I wonder if the fairies will need our help again today!"

Fairy in Hiding

The girls scattered some more feed around the meadow.

"I hope you enjoy your meal," said Kirsty, smiling at the deer.

"It's nice to meet some humans who really understand us," said a handsome buck. "The others who work here are very nice, but they don't always seem to know what we want."

“Do you like living at the reserve?” asked Rachel.

“It’s wonderful here,” said the buck. “All the food we can eat, and huge, tree-filled areas to live in. It’s perfect.”

The girls smiled, and Kirsty took off her blue-and-white sun hat and wiped her forehead. The day was getting hotter and hotter. The hat slipped out of her hand and fell onto the ground. Before Kirsty could pick it up, the handsome buck had stepped on it by accident.

“I’m very

sorry," he said, lifting his hoof. "I hope I didn't mess it up."

"Oh, no, it's fine," said Kirsty. She picked it up and hooked it over a twig on a tree at the edge of the woods for safekeeping.

Rachel was gazing around at the deer who were happily feeding. A different buck gently nudged her with his antlers. "There seems to be a little more food in that bucket . . ." he remarked.

Rachel laughed and bent down to empty the rest of the food onto the grass. As she straightened

up, she saw something move among the trees in front of her.

"Kirsty, look over there," she whispered. "I think it's the baby fawn that Becky was talking about."

Both girls gazed over and saw a small, dappled fawn that was trying to hide behind a tree.

"Oh, he's shy," said Kirsty.

She held out her hand and walked toward the fawn.

“Leave some for the others, OK?” Rachel said to the buck with a grin.

She followed Kirsty toward the trees.

“There’s some tasty food over here,” Kirsty said in a soft voice. “Why don’t you come and try some?”

The little fawn took a few steps back.

“There’s plenty to go around,” said Rachel.

But the fawn hid his face behind a large bush.

“Don’t be scared,” said Kirsty in a kind voice.

At that moment, Rachel heard a faint, tinkling voice. She put her hand on Kirsty's arm.

"Listen!" she said.

"Rachel!" came the voice again. "Kirsty!"

"It's a fairy!" said Kirsty.

The girls looked around, trying to follow the sound of the voice.

"It's coming from your sun hat!" said Rachel.

They ran over to the tree where Kirsty had hung her hat, but there was no one there.

"I'm sure that it came from over here," said Rachel, feeling confused.

They heard a tiny giggle.

"It's nice to see you again," said the voice.

Kirsty stared more closely at her hat, and then a big smile spread across her face.

"It's Savannah the Zebra Fairy!" she said.

It was no wonder that they could hardly see Savannah against the blue-and-white stripes of the hat. The fairy was wearing a blue-striped tunic dress with dark leggings. Savannah's reddish-brown hair glinted in the sunlight as she hovered in front of them.

“Hello, Savannah!” said Rachel in an excited voice. “We almost didn’t see you.”

“My stripes camouflage me,” said Savannah, turning a little pirouette against the backdrop of the hat. “None of the human visitors can see me, even though I’m in full view. I blend right in!”

“That’s amazing,” said Kirsty, looking at all the visitors. “Some of them are looking right at you, Savannah. That’s so clever.”

“I learned it from my friends the zebras,” said Savannah. “They have stripes that camouflage them on the grassy plains.”

“It would be amazing to see a real zebra,” said Rachel.

“Actually, I’ve come to ask if you’d like

to see some right now," said Savannah. "You see, there are some goblins chasing them, and they're getting scared . . . I would really appreciate your help."

"We'll come right away!" said Kirsty.

Stampede!

"We'll do anything we can to stop Jack Frost and his goblins," said Rachel.

The girls glanced back at the deer. They were finishing the food the girls had scattered. Becky was still talking to the visitors, and no one was looking at the girls. They slipped behind the tree where the fawn had hidden.

Savannah lifted her wand and waved it over the girls in a zigzag pattern. Instantly, they felt the power of Savannah's magic sweep them into the air, and the trees around them disappeared.

"I feel as if I've walked into a sauna," said Kirsty, looking around. "Wow, where are we?"

They were standing on a grassy plain. It stretched so far in all directions that the girls couldn't see where it ended or began. The sky was bright blue, and everything shimmered in the heat.

"What's that noise?" asked Rachel.

Savannah and Kirsty listened. They could hear a thundering roar, which seemed to be getting louder. Then Kirsty turned around and yelled.

"Stampede!"

A herd of zebras was pounding toward them across the plain!

Savannah waved her wand again and the girls were transformed into fairies. In the blink of an eye, they were zooming upward. Their wings fluttered so fast that they were blurry with speed.

They were just in time! The fairies felt a rush of air as the herd of zebras charged underneath them.

"Look!" cried Rachel, pointing to the back of the stampede.

A baby zebra was scampering along, trying to keep up.

"He looks scared," said Savannah. "Come on, let's go and see him."

She led Rachel and Kirsty over the crowd of zebras until they were flying alongside the baby zebra.

"Hello, little one," said Savannah. "These are my friends Rachel and Kirsty. Why are you all running?"

"I'm Ziggy," said the little zebra in a breathless voice. "Haven't you seen the strange green things? They're scary!"

Two adult zebras slowed down and trotted back to Ziggy.

"Mom, Dad!" cried Ziggy. "I'm glad to see you! Look, I made some new friends!"

"Ziggy, you have to stay with the herd," said his mother. "It's dangerous to be alone when those strange creatures are around."

"What were they like?" asked Savannah.

"There were four of them," said Ziggy's father. "Green creatures with enormous feet and long noses."

Rachel and Kirsty exchanged a suspicious glance.

“That sounds like goblins,” said Rachel.

“Maybe if we follow the zebras’ hoofprints back the way they came, we can find the goblins,” said Kirsty.

“Great plan!” Savannah said, turning around with a determined expression.

The three friends rose high above the grassy plain, following the zebras’ hoofprints in the other direction. They flew a long way, tracking the prints back across the grass. They flew over wide-spreading trees. Finally, Rachel called out.

“Look—down there!” she cried.

Two goblins were sitting beside a watering hole, holding a big brown sack.

The girls fluttered down and hid in the long grass around the watering

hole. The goblins were talking loudly, not thinking that anyone could be listening.

"We have to catch the baby zebra before the other two," said the shorter goblin.

"Who is he talking about?" asked

Rachel in a whisper. "Who else would be trying to catch Ziggy?"

"Ziggy's parents said that they had seen four green creatures," Kirsty remembered. "There must be two more goblins around here somewhere. Maybe they're having a competition to see who can catch Ziggy first."

"Those mean goblins!" said Savannah.

"The others have that fairy's key chain toy to help them catch the zebra," said the tall goblin in a gloomy voice. "We don't stand a chance."

"Don't be silly," said the short goblin. "We have a bag full of zebra traps, and all they have is that little fluffy toy."

He opened the sack and pulled out a large net, herbs and twigs to attract the zebra, and a rope tied at the end like a lasso.

"Jack Frost will be very pleased with us when we bring him that baby zebra," the short goblin continued. "He'll probably give us a big reward."

Kirsty put her hand over her mouth, looking upset.

"They're planning to use those horrible things to catch Ziggy!" she said in a low voice. "We have to stop them!"

A Zany Zebra

Rachel was thinking about Ziggy running along with his family. Suddenly, she had an idea.

"Savannah, can you use magic to make the sound of a zebra stampede?" she asked. "If we can make the goblins think that they hear the zebras, maybe we can lure them away from where Ziggy really is."

"That's a great idea," said Savannah.

She waved her wand, and suddenly the girls heard the thunder of zebra hooves. The sound was coming from the opposite direction of where the zebras had really gone.

"Listen!" said the tall goblin, sitting up very straight. "That's the zebras—it's coming from over there! Come on!"

They stuffed their equipment back into the sack and ran off with it—far away from the zebras!

Rachel, Kirsty, and Savannah burst into laughter.

"That's two goblins out of the way," said Kirsty.

"Which leaves two more to find, as well as Savannah's key chain," said Rachel.

"Let's go back and check on Ziggy," Savannah suggested.

The three friends zoomed up, enjoying the warmth of the sun on their wings. They flew back across the grassy plain to the zebras. The herd had stopped running, and they were grazing on the juicy grass.

Kirsty and Rachel spiraled down, followed by Savannah.

"All I can see is black and white," said Rachel with a laugh.

“And green,” said Kirsty in a worried voice. “Look at that zebra over there. It has *green*-and-white stripes!”

The strange-looking zebra was in the center of the herd, moving steadily toward Ziggy and his parents.

Savannah frowned and waved her wand. All their outfits changed, and they were now each wearing a black-and-white tunic dress.

“The stripes will help to camouflage us,” the little fairy explained. “Come on—we have to save Ziggy!”

They swooped down and landed on Ziggy’s back. But he didn’t seem to notice them. He was moving through the crowd of zebras, faster and faster, leaving his parents behind. Rachel stood up on his back and peered ahead.

"He's moving toward the green-and-white zebra," she said.

Kirsty stood up, too, and she and Rachel held hands. Ziggy was galloping now, and they had to flutter their wings to keep their balance.

"Look at the green zebra's feet," said Savannah. "They're enormous!"

They were very close now. Suddenly they heard a grumbling voice coming from the back end of the zebra.

"What's going on?" said the voice. "Haven't you caught that zebra yet?"

“That’s not a zebra,” said Rachel. “It’s two goblins in disguise!”

There was a muffled squawk from the front end of the zebra.

“The goblin at the front must have something in his mouth,” said Rachel.

“I bet it’s Savannah’s magic key chain,” said Kirsty in excitement. “That must be why Ziggy’s following the green-and-white zebra. The goblins are using Savannah's special charm to get Ziggy away from the herd."

"How are we going to get it back from inside a zebra costume?" asked Savannah.

She sounded defeated. Rachel and Kirsty squeezed her hands.

"I have an idea," said Kirsty. "If all the zebras go for a drink at the watering hole, the goblin zebra will have to open its mouth to drink . . ."

"And it'll drop the key chain," finished Rachel. "Awesome idea, Kirsty!"

"But how can we get the zebras to go for a drink?" Kirsty asked. "Can you cast a spell, Savannah?"

Savannah laughed.

"There's no need for magic," she said.

"The zebras are our friends. All we have to do is ask."

The girls split up and flitted among the zebras, asking each one to head to the watering hole. They flew low and stayed close to the zebras so the goblins didn't spot them. A few minutes later, the whole herd set off for the watering hole. At first they trotted and then they started to run, their hooves pounding and shaking the ground. They ran faster and faster, and soon only two zebras were lagging behind—the goblin zebra . . . and Ziggy.

By the time the goblins reached the watering hole, most of the other zebras had already finished drinking. The front goblin trotted up to the hole. As soon as it dipped its head, Savannah's magic key chain dropped into the shallow water.

"There it is!" said Kirsty. "Come on!"

The three fairies swooped off Ziggy's back and darted down to the water, but then a hand reached out from the middle of the zebra costume. It was the goblin who was disguised as the back legs of the zebra, and he snatched the zebra charm from under their hands.

"Fairies!" he yelled. "Pesky fairies! RUN!"

The front goblin panicked and ran in one direction, while the back goblin darted another way.

"This way!" squealed the front goblin.

The pretend zebra stumbled off across the grassland, followed by Ziggy.

"Ziggy, come back!" cried Rachel.

The fairies flew after them at top speed.

"Even if we catch those rotten goblins, how can we stop them?" asked Kirsty.

"I wish we had the lasso those other goblins had!" Rachel puffed.

Savannah grinned and waved her wand. Instantly, a long lasso appeared in Rachel's hands.

"Fabulous!" said Rachel.

With Kirsty and Savannah holding the other end of the rope, Rachel whirled the lasso in the air and then aimed it at the goblin zebra. Could she make the throw?

Rachel flung the lasso over the pretend zebra's front end and pulled it tight. Then she flew around and coiled the

rope around its back legs. She'd captured the goblins! Frightened, Ziggy gave a cry of alarm and ran back to his parents and the herd. The goblins struggled in the lasso, and the pretend zebra head came off and flopped to one side. Underneath was a very hot, very angry-looking goblin. He wiggled, but his arms were trapped at his sides by the lasso.

"Let us go!" he squawked. "You'll be sorry if you don't!"

“You can’t scare us with your threats,” Kirsty replied.

The back end of the green-and-white zebra wiggled from side to side.

“I can’t move!” came a muffled wail from the zebra’s bottom. “Set my legs free!”

“Give us back Savannah’s key chain first,” said Rachel. “Then we’ll let you go.”

The goblins both stuck out their tongues and scowled in reply.

“All right,” said Rachel. “We can’t force you to give the key chain back. But we can’t let you hurt Ziggy, either. So we’ll just have to tie you up until we can be sure that Ziggy is safe.”

She winked at Kirsty and Savannah,

and started to wind the rope around the goblins some more.

"Stop that!" shrieked the front goblin.

"I can't move!" wailed the goblin in back. "Let us go!"

"Give Savannah her magic key chain and then you can go free," said Rachel.

"Jack Frost will be so angry if we go back without the zebra," cried the back goblin.

"He'll be even angrier if we don't go back at all," said the front goblin.

"Besides, it's lunchtime and I'm hungry. Give the silly fairy what she wants and let's get out of here."

Making loud grumbling noises, the back goblin put one hand out of the bottom of the costume and threw the magic zebra charm at Savannah. She caught it, and it returned to fairy-size at once.

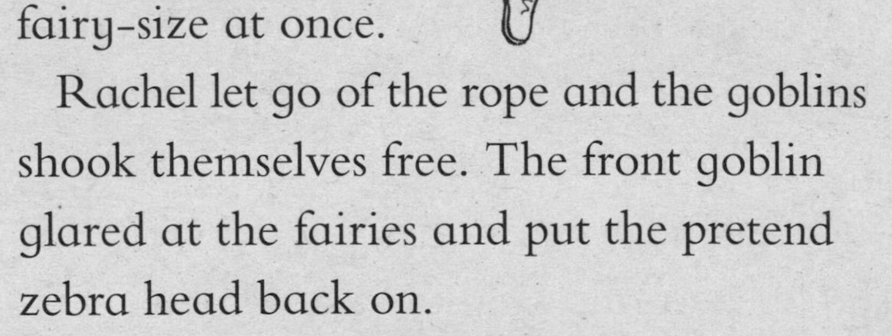

Rachel let go of the rope and the goblins shook themselves free. The front goblin glared at the fairies and put the pretend zebra head back on.

"Let's get back to the Ice Castle," he said. "I'm sick of zebras, and I'm sick of fairies."

The goblins staggered away, still in their green-and-white costume.

"Let's go and make sure Ziggy's OK," said Savannah.

The three fairies zipped back to the watering hole, where all the zebras were waiting for them. Savannah fluttered over to Ziggy, who was breathing heavily. She stroked his velvety muzzle and whispered to him. Steadily, his breathing slowed down and he started to look happier.

Ziggy's mother trotted over to where Rachel and Kirsty were hovering in the air.

"Thank you so much for helping to protect my son," she said. "We will never forget what you did for us today."

The whole herd gave the fairies three cheers, and then Savannah put her arms around Rachel and Kirsty.

"It's time for you to go back to the nature reserve," she said. "There are animals there who need you, too."

Kirsty and Rachel couldn't wait to get back to Wild Woods. The deer would be waiting for them!

A Magic Touch

Savannah waved her wand. In the blink of an eye, the girls found themselves behind the tree in the meadow at Wild Woods Nature Reserve. Rachel and Kirsty looked around. The deer were still eating, the visitors were still listening to Becky's talk, and the cute little fawn was still too shy to come out from behind the trees. Kirsty reached up and took her hat down from the tree.

"No time has passed since you left," said Savannah. "No one noticed anything. Girls, I can't thank you enough for helping me to find my magic key chain. It will really cheer up the other Baby Animal Rescue Fairies to hear what happened today."

"Are you going back to Fairyland now?" Kirsty asked.

Savannah nodded. "I'm so happy that the zebras are safe," she said. "I hope you enjoy the rest of the week here, girls."

Savannah gave the girls a tiny kiss and then raised her wand. She made a zigzag in the air, and black-and-white fairy dust fell all around her. When the sparkles cleared, she had disappeared.

"I'm so glad that we were able to help Savannah," said Rachel. "I just wish that we could help that shy little fawn, too."

"Maybe we can," said Kirsty. "Remember how Savannah calmed Ziggy down?"

She turned to the fawn, who trem as she stepped closer to him.

"Hello," she said. "My name's Kirsty."

She reached out her hand and very, very gently stroked his nose. The fawn shifted his feet around, but he seemed to like the attention.

Kirsty said in a soft

iends. All those

you are your

The fawn tilted his head to one side, then nibbled at her sun hat. Kirsty giggled and pulled it away from him. Rachel fetched a handful of feed and held it out to him.

"Come on," she said in a gentle voice. "Come into the open."

Slowly, Rachel and Kirsty led the little fawn out into the meadow. Step by step, he moved closer to the fence, nibbling tasty treats from Rachel's hand as he walked.

The visitors had noticed what the girls were doing, and were watching in breathless silence. The little fawn looked over at all the curious faces staring at him. He looked at Rachel and Kirsty, and they gave him reassuring smiles and nods. The fawn's head went up, and then he trotted over to the fence to say hello to the visitors.

"You two have a magic touch with animals," said Becky, walking over to them. "No one else has been able to get that little fawn into the open."

Rachel and Kirsty shared a secret smile. Becky had no idea that she was speaking the absolute truth!

"Thank you for doing such a wonderful job this morning," Becky went on. "Here are your badges."

She handed each of them a badge with a picture of a deer to put on their backpacks.

“Thank you!” said the girls together.

As they walked across the meadow to pick up the empty feed buckets, Rachel squeezed her best friend’s hand.

“I wonder what kind of animal we’ll be helping next,” she said.

"Whatever it is, it'll be amazing," Kirsty replied. "I can't wait!"

Rachel grinned in response. This week at Wild Woods Nature Reserve was turning out to be one of their best vacations yet!

THE BABY ANIMAL RESCUE FAIRIES

Rachel and Kirsty found Mae, Kitty, Mara, and Savannah's missing magic key chains. Now it's time for them to help

Kimberly
the Koala Fairy!

Join their next adventure in this special sneak peek . . .

"So, here we are again at Wild Woods. Maybe we'll get another badge today," Kirsty Tate said hopefully, smiling at her best friend, Rachel Walker.

The girls were outside the wildlife center with the other junior rangers. They were all waiting for Becky, the head of the Wild Woods Nature Reserve. Rachel and Kirsty had volunteered to spend a week of summer vacation working at the reserve, which was near Kirsty's home. Every day, Becky gave the junior rangers a job to do. If they successfully completed the tasks, they each received a badge.

"It would be *amazing* to get another one!" Rachel exclaimed, patting her backpack proudly. The girls' hard work had already earned them four badges, and they'd pinned them to the pockets of their backpacks. "It's great to know that we're helping wildlife, and it's really fun, too."

"And helping out at Wild Woods isn't our *only* job this week," Kirsty reminded Rachel. "We're helping the Baby Animal Rescue Fairies, too!"

"I wonder if we'll help rescue another

baby animal today," Rachel murmured. "The four we've met so far have all been so cute!"

Becky came out of the wildlife center, holding a clipboard in one hand and a bag of equipment in the other. "Morning, everyone," she called cheerfully. "I have lots of jobs for you today." She consulted her clipboard, then smiled at Rachel and Kirsty. "OK, girls, you're first. Follow me!"

HIT entertainment